THE RED JACKET

Written and illustrated by **Bob Holt**

HARPER
An Imprint of HarperCollinsPublishers

WOULD YOU
LIKE A
RED JACKET?

ARE YOU
TALKING TO
ME?

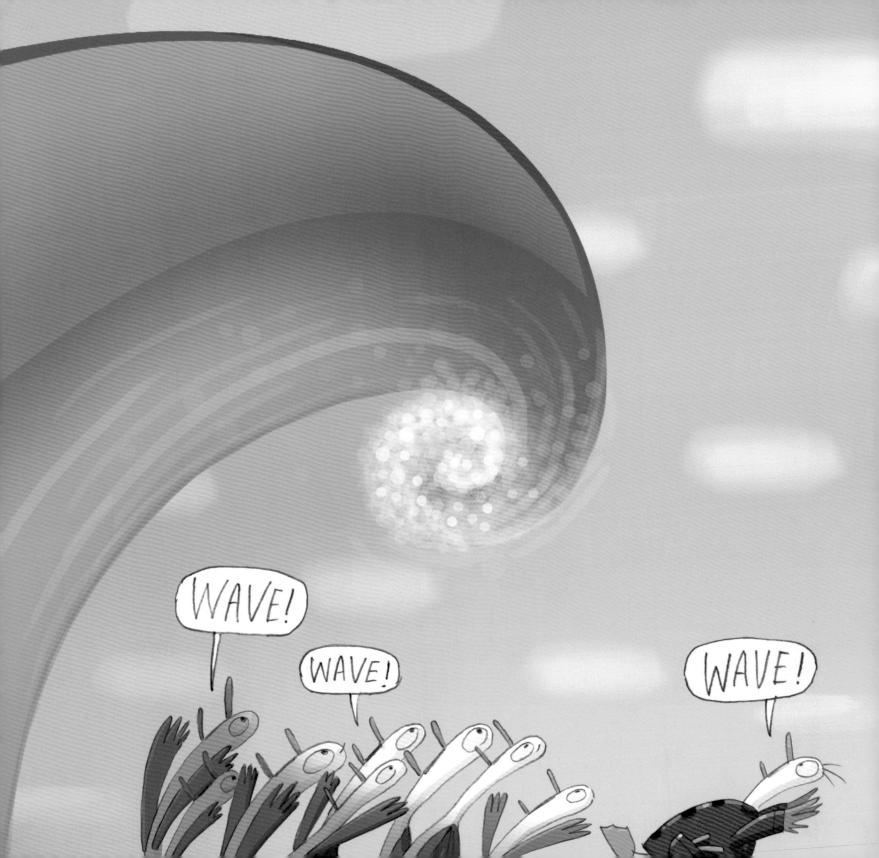

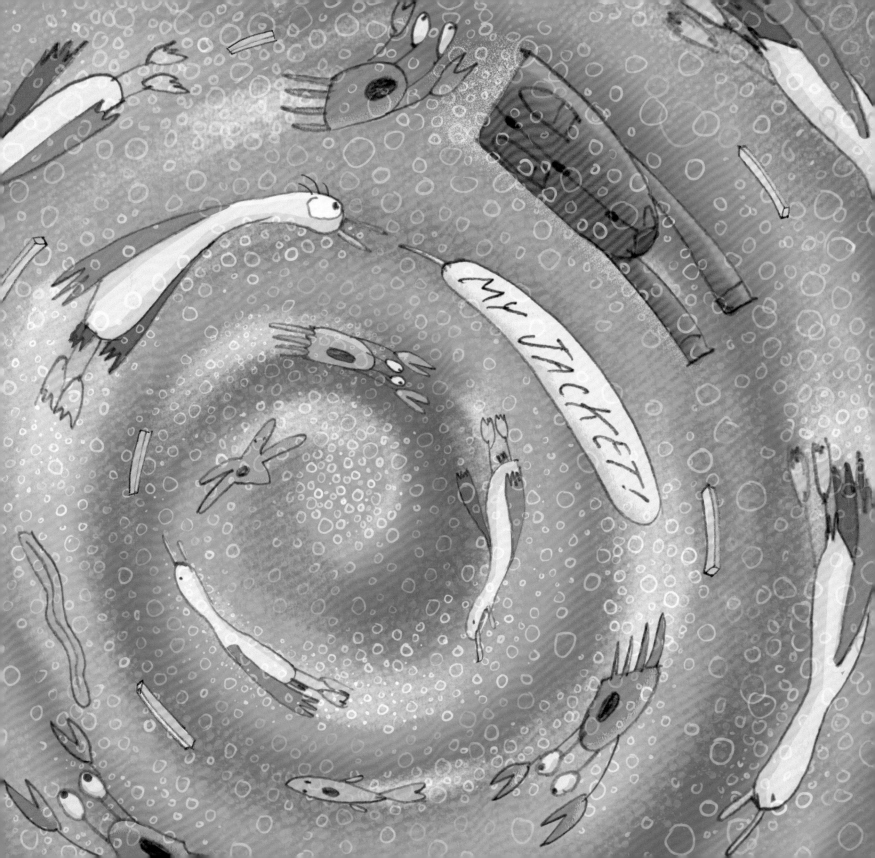

HEY.
BOB.

WE FOUND
YOUR RED JACKET.

HOW?

Dedicated to Margie Blumberg, who convinced
me that I could write children's books.
Thanks for the red jacket, Margie.

The Red Jacket
Copyright © 2023 by Bob Holt
All rights reserved. Manufactured in Italy.
No part of this book may be used or reproduced in any manner whatsoever
without written permission except in the case of brief quotations embodied in
critical articles and reviews. For information address HarperCollins Children's Books,
a division of HarperCollins Publishers, 195 Broadway, New York, NY 10007.
www.harpercollinschildrens.com

Library of Congress Control Number: 2022938134
ISBN 978-0-06-323760-5

The artist used pencil drawings digitally painted
to create the illustrations for this book.
Book design by Rachel Zegar
23 24 25 26 27 RTLO 10 9 8 7 6 5 4 3 2 1
First Edition